Maxwell's Magic Mix-Up

by Linda Ashman

illustrated by Regan Dunnick

Simon & Schuster Books for Young Readers

New York London Toronto Sydney Singapore

SIMON & SCHUSTER BOOKS FOR YOUNG READERS
An imprint of Simon & Schuster Children's Publishing Division
1230 Avenue of the Americas, New York, New York 10020
Text copyright © 2001 by Linda Ashman
Illustrations copyright © 2001 by Regan Dunnick
SIMON & SCHUSTER BOOKS FOR YOUNG READERS is a trademark of Simon & Schuster.
Book design by Paul Zakris
The text of this book is set in 16-point Else Semi Bold.
The illustrations are rendered in mixed media.
Printed in Hong Kong
10 9 8 7 6 5 4 3 2 1

Library of Congress Cataloging-in-Publication Data
Ashman, Linda.
Maxwell's magic mix-up / by Linda Ashman ;
illustrated by Regan Dunnick. — 1st ed.   p.   cm.
Summary: A faulty magician creates
quite an uproar at a party when he turns
the birthday girl into a rock and the
guests into different animals.
ISBN 0-689-83178-1
[1. Magicians—Fiction. 2. Parties—Fiction.
3. Birthdays—Fiction. 4. Stories in rhyme.]
I. Dunnick, Regan, ill.
II. Title.
PZ8.3.H5344Ho 2001
[E]—dc21
99-39431
CIP

To my mother, Joyce,
and in memory of my father, Vince, with much love
—L. A.

To my family,
and to Whiskers,
the hairless cat I never really knew
—R. D.

it's my sister's seventh birthday.
Entertainer calls in sick.
Poor Louise is brokenhearted.
Better find a backup quick!

Call the ghost, the clown, the dragon.
Call the circus and the zoo.
Only Maxwell the Magician
Isn't booked today at two.

Party starts. Magician enters.
Hocus pocus! What a shock!
Stumbles through his incantation . . .

Turns Louise into a rock.

Joey grabs the rock and hollers,
"Look what's happened to Louise!"
Mother thunders at the wizard,
"Don't just stand there! Fix her, *please!*"

Just as Joey starts to throw her,
Maxwell yells a magic word.
All at once, Louise is falling,
Still a rock . . .

Wingabinga!

But Joe's a bird.

Joey's flying skills are dismal.
Swoops and falters in midair.
Hits a lamp shade, tumbles over,
Snags a claw in Katie's hair.

"Get him off me!" clamors Katie.

Maxwell bows and taps his hat.
In an instant, Joe's untangled.

Too bad Kate is now a cat.

Kate the cat is eyeing Joey.
Seems to think he's kitty chow.
"Katie, no!" I say. "It's Joey!"
Katie stares and says, "Meeeeooow."

"Fix these children!" yells my father.
Chases Max around the room.
"Yes, of course!" the wizard sputters.

Turns my dad into a broom.

I can tell my father's angry.
For a broom, he looks quite mean.
He is sweeping like a demon.
Never seen the floor so clean.

"My turn! My turn!" pesters Peter.
"Turn me into something BIG!"
"At your service," Maxwell answers.
Blinks an eye . . .

And Pete's a pig.

Pete is charging toward the kitchen.
Doesn't pause to take a break.
He inhales a plate of cookies.
Eyes Louise's birthday cake.

"Not the birthday cake!" says Mother.
Maxwell spins and waves a hand.
Cake is spared, the pig diverted . . .

By a ten-piece marching band.

"I give up!" the wizard whimpers.
"Doesn't seem to be my day."
Grabs the phone and calls his office.
"Please send Alex right away!"

Band is playing marching music.
Dad is sweeping to the beat.
Joe is flying high above us.
Kate is purring at our feet.

Mom is sobbing. Max is pacing.
Pete is eating chips and cheese.
In the midst of all this chaos
Sits the birthday rock, Louise.

Doorbell rings. A child enters.
"Who are you?" my mother cries.
"I am here to help my uncle.
Call me Al," the boy replies.

Maxwell rushes to his nephew.
Says, "I missed a trick or two."
Alex sighs and says, "No kidding.
Let me see what I can do."

Alex crouches down before us,
Barely breathing, in a trance.
Then he orders, "Start the music!"
And begins a wild dance.

Shakes his head and shrugs his shoulders,
Leaps and lunges, skips and hops.
Claps his hands and yells, "Reverse it!"
In a flash, the music stops.

Joe is hanging from a streamer.
Dad is propped against the door.
Kate is curled up on a bookshelf.
Pete is sprawling on the floor.

"Back to normal," Al announces.
"Oh, thank heaven!" Maxwell sighs.
Pack their bags and start to exit.
"Not so fast!" my mother cries.

"Quite a show!" she tells the duo.
"Simply brilliant! Splendid! Grand!
But you missed one tiny detail."

Mother reaches out her hand.

"Not the rock trick, Uncle Maxwell!"
Al is gasping. "Is it true?"
Maxwell nods. His nephew cringes.
"That's the hardest to undo!"

Alex takes Louise from Mother.
Sets her down beside the clock.
"Time go backward!" Alex orders,

But Louise remains a rock.

"She's a stubborn one," says Alex.
"Metamorphic, I suspect."
Runs in circles, chanting loudly,
But his spell has no effect.

AAAhchOoo!

Al collapses on the sofa.
Bows his head as if to doze.
Tiny feather floating by him
Passes right beneath his nose.

"There's a tickle in my nostril."
Al *aaaaachoooos!* a giant sneeze.
Spills a soda on my sister,

And the rock becomes Louise.

Mother hugs her. Father blubbers,
"Oh, you're back, my little pet!"
But Louise just yawns and mutters,
"Is it time for presents yet?"

"What a party!" say the neighbors.
"Great magician! Best in town!"
Still I think that for my birthday,

I would rather have a clown.